Iktomi
and the
Buzzard

Hi, kids! I'M IKTOMI! —and proud of it! Don't read this book. That white guy, Paul Goble, is stealing my stories and making money off of them. This book is ethnically insensitive material about me; its racial epithets just bring me into contempt, ridicule, and disrepute. Hey! You're G·R·E·A·T kids! I've got my rights, I have. I don't have to put up with his derogatory, disreputable, disparaging, and denigrating slurs and offensive designations. I'm being victimized. I have always been here on this Turtle Continent, and I'll be the last here, long after all white people have been forgotten. I'm no racist, but I'm excited just thinking about it! I'm nobody's football or baseball mascot! I was the first enrolled member of the Great Lakota Sioux Nation, born in Nihil, South Dakota, and etc. and etc. and etc. . . . .

Iktomi
and the
Buzzard

a Plains Indian story

told and illustrated
by PAUL GOBLE

Orchard Books   New York

for Janet and Robert,
with all my love

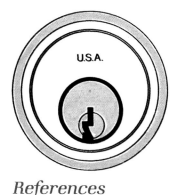

References

Deloria, Ella C., *Dakota Texts* ("Ikto and the Raccoon Skin"), Vol. 14, Publications of the American Ethnological Society, New York, 1932. Dorsey, George Amos, *The Pawnee: Mythology* ("Coyote-Man and His Tricks"), Part I, Publications of the Carnegie Institution, LIX, Washington, D.C., 1906. *Traditions of the Skidi Pawnee* ("Animal Stories"), Memoirs of the American Folk-lore Society, VIII, Boston and New York, 1904. Dorsey, James Owen, *A Study of Siouan Cults*, Eleventh Annual Report, Bureau of American Ethnology, Washington, D.C., 1894. *Teton Folk-lore Notes* ("Spider Lore"), Journal of American Folk-lore, II, Chicago, 1889. *The Thegiha Language: Myths, Stories, and Letters* ("Ictinike and the Buzzard"), Contributions to North American Ethnology (Smithsonian Institution), VI, Washington, D.C., 1890. Erdoes, Richard, *The Sound of Flutes, and Other Indian Legends* ("Iktome and the Hawk"), Pantheon Books, New York, 1976. Lowie, Robert H., *The Assiniboine*, Anthropological Papers of the American Museum of Natural History, Vol. IV, Part 1, New York, 1909. McClintock, Walter, *The Old North Trail; Life, Legends and Religion of the Blackfeet Indians* ("Old Man Flies with the Cranes"), Macmillan, London, 1910. One Feather, Gerald and Vivian, *Ehanni Ohunkakan* ("Iktomi and the Buzzard"), Red Cloud Indian School, Pine Ridge, 1974. Pratt, Vince E., *The Story of Iktomi (The Spider)*, Featherstone, Agency Village, South Dakota, 1988. Skinner, Alanson, *Plains Ojibwa Tales* ("Nanibozhu and the Buzzard"), The Journal of American Folk-lore, Vol. 32, New York, 1919. Theisz, Ronald, *Buckskin Tokens: Contemporary Oral Narratives of the Lakota*, Sinte Gleska College, Rosebud, 1975. Thompson, Stith, *Tales of the North American Indians*, Indiana University Press, Bloomington, 1929.

Copyright © 1994 by Paul Goble. First Orchard Paperbacks edition 1998. All rights reserved. No part of this book may be reproduced or transmitted in any form or by any means, electronic or mechanical, including photocopying, recording, or by any information storage or retrieval system, without permission in writing from the Publisher. Orchard Books, 95 Madison Avenue, New York, NY 10016. Manufactured in the United States of America. Printed by Barton Press, Inc. Bound by Horowitz/Rae. The text of this book is set in 22 point ITC Zapf Book Light. The illustrations are India ink and watercolor on Oram & Robinson (England) Limited Watercolour Board, reproduced in combined line and halftone. Library of Congress Cataloging-in-Publication Data. Goble, Paul. Iktomi and the buzzard : a Plains Indian story / told and illustrated by Paul Goble. p. cm. "A Richard Jackson book." Includes bibliographical references. Summary: Iktomi the trickster tries to fool a buzzard into carrying him across the river on the buzzard's back. Asides printed in italics may be used by the storyteller to encourage listeners to make their own remarks about the action, as in traditional Iktomi storytelling. ISBN 0-531-06812-9 (tr.) ISBN 0-531-08662-3 (lib. bdg.) ISBN 0-531-07100-6 (pbk.) 1. Indians of North America—Great Plains—Legends. 2. Teton Indians—Legends. 3. Trickster—Great Plains—Juvenile literature. [1. Dakota Indians—Legends. 2. Indians of North America—Great Plains—Legends.] I. Title. E78.G73G628 1994 398.2'089'975—dc20 [E] 93-24872 Hardcover 10 9 8 7 6 5 4 3 2 Paperback 10 9 8 7 6 5 4 3 2 1 Book design by Paul Goble.

About Iktomi

The word *Iktomi* means "spider" in Lakota. It is also the name of their mythological Trickster and helper of the Creator when the world was new. All Native Americans share the same character, calling him by different names. Both Iktomi the spider and Iktomi the Trickster were here long before people, and so they are referred to respectfully as "Grandfather." If you kill a spider, you have to say: "Grandfather Spider, the Thunderbeings kill you!" The spirit of the spider believes it is the lightning which killed him, and so he will not tell other spiders what you have done. In Lakota: "*Iktomi, Tunkashila, Wakinyan niktepelo!*"

Iktomi the Trickster never dies. He is like us: a complex and contradictory mix of godlike and evil possibilities, cleverness and stupidity. He can take on the form of any bird or animal, and yet in this story he cannot change himself into a bird to fly across the river. He can make himself small enough to ride on Buzzard's back; yet he is helpless to make himself small enough to escape from the hollow tree in which Buzzard dumped him.

The closer we try to bring him into focus, the more we lose sight of him. We have the same problem trying to understand ourselves, and each other. Iktomi helps us to laugh, not to cry or give up. In traditional times he reflected the chaotic element in an otherwise ordered society. Today there is little order, and Iktomi seems to reflect life itself. Although revered, the sacred myths are hardly a living part of the spiritual life any longer, but these ancient Trickster stories are still very much alive. New ones have been added to the Trickster's repertoire. They are stories about all of us: are we not like Iktomi, just "walking along," idle, directionless, easily distracted, and ready for the next piece of fashionable nonsense or mischief?

A Note for the Reader

The themes of Iktomi stories are familiar; enjoyment comes from the obvious humor and from hearing them again. The passages printed in the gray type are intended to encourage listeners, young and old, to make comments. Iktomi's thoughts, in the small type, can be read when looking at the pictures. Some readers may like to try singing the songs!

These are stories with a moral, which should be told without moralizing, while we delight in Iktomi's dreadful behavior.

Iktomi was walking along. . . .
*Every story about Iktomi
starts the same way.*

Iktomi was walking along.
He was going to the powwow.
He was wearing his feathers
for the Eagle Dance.

I have an excellent
self-image today.

I bet the kids think
I can't see anything
under this mask.
I can see better than Eagle.

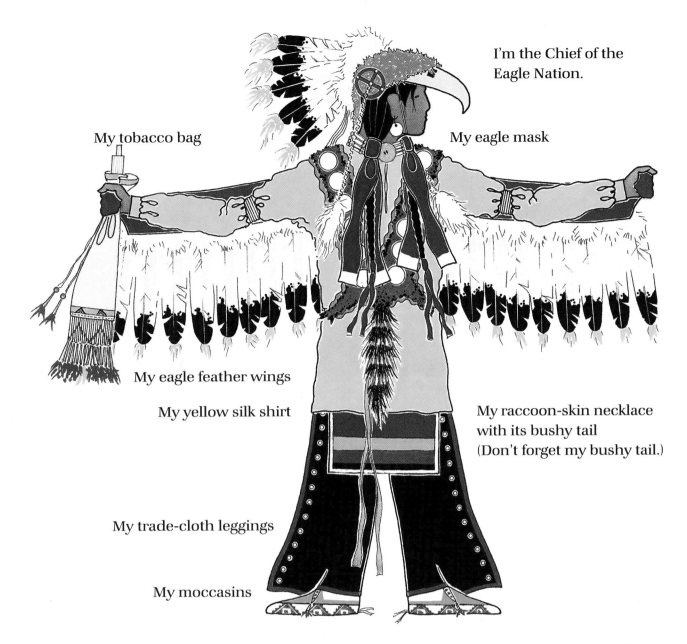

I'm the Chief of the Eagle Nation.

My tobacco bag

My eagle mask

My eagle feather wings

My yellow silk shirt

My raccoon-skin necklace with its bushy tail (Don't forget my bushy tail.)

My trade-cloth leggings

My moccasins

"People like to see me Eagle Dancing,"
he was boasting to himself.
"Sometimes I think I look
just like Eagle.
Sometimes I think I look much better."

Iktomi is such a braggart!
He thinks so much of himself.

I expect Eagle wishes he
had all my feathers.
Am I an endangered species?

Iktomi tried a few dance steps. . . .
"I'm *Wanbli*, the Eagle,
when I wear his feathers.
See me soar above the buttes,
high up, close to Father Sun.
I look down on the whole world!
I glide over the plains.
Look at me, everyone!"

What imagination!

This is Eagle Dancing as my
ancestors did it — except
I do it better.

Iktomi came to a river.
It was much too wide to cross.
Of course he did not want to get
his feathers wet.

He sat down on the bank.
"Whatever shall I do now?"
he wondered.
"My day was going so well. . . .
Now I'll never get to the powwow.
I'll never win all the prize money.
Oh, dear. . . ."

I ought to be a Duck Dancer.

They say Buzzard SMELLS his
prey. . . . Did I forget
my roll-on?

Iktomi spied Buzzard*
circling in the sky.
Hecha, the Buzzard, is forever
making circles in the high above.
He sees everything moving
on the ground.
He had been watching
Iktomi all the while.

You saw Buzzard, didn't you?

* Turkey Vulture — *Cathartes aura*

Iktomi pretended to cry,
but he was watching Buzzard's
reflection in the water.
Between his tears he started singing:
    "I am forever thinking:
        If only—if only
        I could reach the other side!"
He sounded so-o-o terribly sad. . . .

Those aren't real tears, are they?
Iktomi must be plotting something.

He sang it again and again:
    "I am forever thinking:
        If o-n-l-y—if o-n-l-y
        I could reach the other side!"
Buzzard circled lower, and asked:
"Whatever is the matter? Don't cry."
"Ah! Hello, younger brother!"
Iktomi called up to Buzzard.
"You gave me a fright!
I didn't know you were there."
That Iktomi is always telling lies.

He's only
a bird.
He believes
anything
I tell him.

Buzzard is
no sparrow.
I can easily
outwit him.

TO´-KIN   KO-WA´-KA-TAN MA-KA´-NI, E-CHIN´CHIN NA-WA´-ZHIN!
I STAND, THINKING OFTEN, OH THAT I MIGHT REACH THE OTHER SIDE!

Iktomi said to Buzzard:
"My dear younger brother,
I know it would grieve you
to see me get my feathers wet.
Therefore, would you, please,
be so very kind as to
transport me across this
fluently flowing effusion of fluidity
—this river?"

What language!
How polite Iktomi is —
when he wants something!

"Well, yes, older brother, of course,"
said good-natured Buzzard.
"Get on my back and I will carry
you to the other side."

My command of the English
language impresses him.
English . . . not American. . . .
Grandmother spoke Lakota.

Funny . . . I've got
a tobacco bag
like the ducks have.
Where is it?

Iktomi had once taken lessons
from a medicine man,
and so he remembered
part of a magic song
to make himself smaller.
He climbed on to Buzzard's back
and sat astride his shoulders.

Iktomi was in such a hurry
he forgot his eagle feathers!

"Now, take me up high,"
Iktomi told Buzzard.
"I want everyone to see
that I can fly!"

He's wanting to show off, as usual.

I really am clever.

No bridle? No saddle?
I wonder if he has
horse sense.

I'm really on top of
everything today.

He was so excited that
he could not keep still.
"This is just great! I CAN FLY!
Hey! Is there anyone down there?
Look at me! I'M IKTOMI!"

Just at that very moment Iktomi noticed that Buzzard did not have any feathers on his head.

I bet the kids want to make this rude sign!!

"How extraordinary . . ."
he thought. "Not a single feather!
Just red skin!"
Iktomi was so amused
that he almost fell off laughing
to himself.
He made rude signs
behind Buzzard's head.
"Old baldy red skin!"
he chuckled to himself,
and thinking he could not be seen,
he amused himself making
insulting gestures at Buzzard.

*Do you think Buzzard knows what
Iktomi is up to?*

Buzzard sees everything which
moves on the earth below him.

Remember?

Buzzard was watching
his shadow on the ground,
and so he saw everything
Iktomi was doing.
He saw his rude gestures.
"The scoundrel,"
Buzzard muttered to himself.
"I should have guessed.
I'll have my revenge
on the rascal."

*What do you think he should do
to Iktomi?*

Thank goodness Buzzard can't
see me!

Buzzard circled
slowly around, and around,
always higher, and higher.

What happened?
Did we hit a cloud?
Oh — HELLLP!

I hope people
aren't watching —
but they'll think
I'm flying.

I'm not ready
to die today. . . .

Did I pay
last month's rent?

Don't just twitter!
For goodness' sake,
SAVE ME!

He had seen a hollow tree,
and was thinking:
"I'll drop Ikto inside that tree."
He took careful aim . . .
and suddenly tipped his wings,
and off fell Iktomi!
DOWN down down down down

"BUZZARD!!!!" Iktomi screamed.
"WHERE are you?? SAVE ME!!"

The birds saw Iktomi falling.
"Oh, look! It's Ikto!" they twittered.
"Oh, poor Ikto! He cannot fly!
DO something, somebody!"
they chittered and chattered.
"Quickly!"

Iktomi fell down inside
the hollow tree.
He was still alive, but stuck fast;
no hope of getting out. . . .

Is this the last of the books
about Iktomi?
Is this where he dies?

"That . . . BLANKETY . . . Buzzard,"
Iktomi thought.
"I just pray that he falls
out of the sky.
Hmmmmmmmmmmmm . . ."

What a horrible way to die.
Won't someone put an end
to my suffering?

And I never picked
out my casket.

The hollow tree belonged
to the Woodpeckers.
They peeped in at Iktomi
through a hole.
"Friends," said Iktomi, "make this
hole bigger and get me out of here."
The Woodpeckers worked hard.
They picked and pecked
at the hole, but they could NOT
peck it large enough
to get Iktomi out.
They gave up and flew away.

Oh, come on!
Work at it,
can't you?
I can do better
than that
with my teeth.

"I shall surely die here.
This is where my poor bones
will lie. . . .
Nobody will ever know my grave."

Just then Iktomi heard voices—
Yes!
Peering through his peephole,
he spied two girls with axes
gathering firewood.
"Ah, what luck!" he thought.
He poked the bushy tail
of his raccoon-skin necklace
out through the Woodpeckers' hole.
Then he sang
in a high-pitched voice:
    "I'm a fat bushy-tailed raccoon
      Sitting here—sitting here.
      Get me out—get me out
      And you'll have lots of grease."

I like girls!
Girls LIKE me!!
What a good thing
my wife isn't here.

"Did you hear?"
one of the girls asked.
"He says he's a fat raccoon in there
and we'll get lots of grease."
"Yes!" said the other. "That's good.
We need lots of grease
for tanning hides."

Girls!
They always
fall in with
my ideas.

She pulled my bushy tail!!

Girls believe anything
I tell them.

She pulled at the raccoon tail,
but Iktomi quickly jerked it back
inside the tree.
He sang again:
>"I'm a fat bushy-tailed raccoon
>   Sitting here — sitting here.
>   Get me out — get me out
>   And you'll have lots of grease."

The girls chopped at the tree:
>   chip-CHOP — chop-CHIP
>   chip-CHOP — chop-CHIP

in time to Iktomi's singing.

When the tree fell down,
Iktomi clambered out.
"Whatever did you women
do that for?" he asked angrily.
"That was my house!
Just LOOK what you've done. . . ."
The girls ran away in a great fright.

Laughing to himself,
and very glad to be free,
Iktomi went on his way again.

Let me think —
Girls distract me —
WHAT was I going to do?

An eagle feather!
I should make another
dance outfit.

*Can anyone guess what Ikto will
get up to next?*